A DOG CALLED DUNKEL

More than anything, Seppala wanted to stand among the men of the valley as the proud master of a magnificent pure-bred Alsatian. But the only dog he could claim was Dunkel — a stray mongrel and a scruffy, irrepressible nuisance.

Maybe he could work in the Kraut stall — or win the Sausage Tree contest — Seppala was sure he'd find a way to buy the Alsatian. But everywhere Seppala went Dunkel trailed after, barking and leaping, upsetting stacks of cabbage, potted flowers, rabbit cages — and Seppala's chances.

Or so Seppala thought. . . .

This warmhearted narrative would be engaging in any setting. But in an atmosphere so genuinely Alsace-Lorraine, with its festival tables brimming over with Kuchen and Schmierkäse, it has added dimension. There is a captivating mood and spirit which Alain heightens in his entrancing illustrations. Indeed, Alsace-Lorraine provides more than a background; its traditions and values are an integral part of the story.

A DOG

by Dale Fife

Coward-McCann   New York

CALLED
DUNKEL

pictures by   alain

To Malcolm Franklin

Text © 1966 by Dale Fife

Pictures © 1966 by Alain

Library of Congress Catalog Card Number: 66-13136

Printed in the United States of America

06209

The last twist of the forest path brought Seppala out of the firs and pines into the sloping meadow high above Storkheim. He waited, ankle deep in yellow Primel and Schneeglöckchen, calling his Cousin Claus, who as usual trailed behind.

If Claus did not hurry they would miss seeing the dog, the big Alsatian Seppala secretly pretended was his own — his own to show off at the Tannenbaum Inn on Herren Sonntag, that special Sunday for men only and their trained dogs.

Seppala adjusted the bundle of firewood strapped to his shoulders. He turned toward the forest again. "Hal-lo Claus," he called. "Hal-lo."

"Hal-lo," the mountains echoed.

Hands on hips, feet firmly on the sloping path, Seppala squinted down into the village, searching for the Widow Weiler and the Alsatian harnessed to the blue two-wheeled cart.

Every workday the widow walked along the cobblestone street, stopping at the homes of the weavers to collect the noon dinners which wives or mothers had prepared. She placed the casseroles and coffeepots in the blue cart, smothering them in a feather bed. When the weavers streamed out of the factory at noon, the widow and the dog were waiting with the steaming dinners.

5

The crystal mountain air made everything in the village below stand out clearly — the rosy roofs snuggled around the sandstone church, the storks standing guard in the nest on the steeple and, yes . . . there was the widow in long skirts, white starched apron billowing about her waist, scarf tied around her head. Already she and the dog were crossing the bridge over the pebbly brook to the factory on the other side.

The bells in the Storkheim church tower began to ring the Angelus.

The chapel bell from Tannenbaum tinkled softly.

The Klosterglocke in the Hochwald struck the hour.

The mountain peaks tossed the bell sounds from rim to rim.

It was noon!

In a hurry now, Seppala took the shortcut through terraced vineyards and hop fields.

When he reached the weaving works, the widow was already handing out the casseroles. The yellow bowl with the ceramic chicken on its cover went to the daughter of the seamstress. The brown earthenware dish and the carafe of red wine were for the son of the potato farmer.

The Alsatian, unharnessed now, was being admired by

a ring of young weavers. He sat on his haunches, head proud, ears alert. His honey-colored undercoat, overlaid with rich brown, glistened in the warm sunlight.

Seppala crouched on his heels in line with the noble face. He did not try to pet the dog. The big Alsatian was not his dog. Not yet!

But one day he would be master of this handsome animal with the watchful eyes and the tail carried with the bravado of a wolf. He would find a way. After all, his family needed a dog and a cart . . . Mama to bring home the vegetables from her garden plot at the edge of the village . . . Papa to deliver his wood carvings . . . even the baby, Annalisa, could be pulled in a cart instead of being carried endlessly. Yes, Seppala convinced himself, the dog was practically a necessity.

He heard Claus' whistle and stood up. His cousin, red-cheeked and breathless, sprinted toward the circle. His shirt was dirty, his sleeve torn. "I was running and went headfirst down the path," Claus explained.

Seppala grinned. "Slippery Foot," Seppala said, jokingly. It was his nickname for Claus, who was somewhat of a daredevil — but a clumsy daredevil.

Claus flashed his wide grin, and then both boys turned their attention to the dog and to the talk of the weavers.

"He can run for twenty minutes, carrying an egg in his mouth without so much as cracking the shell," one of the men said admiringly.

"He is the best-trained dog in the valley," another said.

There was a loud yelping from the brook and up the bank leapt Dunkel, the mongrel dog who had been hanging around the village for a week now. He had arrived hungry, limping, with a welt across his back. But now he was filled with life. He jumped up on Seppala, then on Claus. Both boys shook him off. Then he began bounding in circles around the Alsatian, yipping and growling. The big dog paid no attention.

Seeing the two dogs together, it was clear that Dunkel was a tramp without dignity or pride. He had the head of an Alsatian but his hair, dusty and matted, was longer than that of the purebred, and his tail was a collie's plume. Because of his dark coloring, the boys had called him Dunkel.

The weavers laughed at Dunkel's silly antics. The storks left the steeple and flew low to see what the noise was all about.

But the widow frowned. "Who owns this nuisance of a dog?" she asked.

"He's a stray," Seppala answered. "With only a rope around his neck for a collar. I feed him sometimes but he is a tramp and he belongs to no one."

"Well, he acts it," the widow said, giving a signal to the Alsatian. The great dog stood, shook himself elegantly, and walked to the cart.

"Now is your chance to ask if she will sell the dog," Claus whispered.

Seppala was afraid to ask. If the widow said no he would have to give up his dream. But as he watched the Alsatian being harnessed he thought about Herren Sonntag. He saw

8

himself walking into the Tannenbaum Inn with his dog. He would be the envy of every boy in the valley.

Tannenbaum Inn was in the High Forest. Seppala had never been inside the inn, but he and Claus had peeked in its windows often enough. The walls were hung with stuffed bear heads, deer, wild boar. Four cuckoo clocks ticked away the minutes, making a funny racket on the half hour and the hour. The serving girls wore the bright skirts of the national dress, and the wings of their headdresses were like giant butterflies.

It was the favorite Sunday pastime of young couples in the little villages in the valley to climb the mountain paths to the inn. The young men carried walking sticks they had made from tree branches. The young women wore thick-soled shoes and bright sweaters. They sang as they walked. This being Alsace, some sang in German, others in French, but most sang in patois:

> "Uf de Berge isch gut wohne —
> Diodirulla, diodirulla, diodira . . ."

10

But Herren Sonntag was a special day at the inn reserved for men and boys to show off their fine dogs.

The only dogs allowed inside the inn were those that were trained not to beg for food, those that did not growl and could not be provoked into fighting. They lay under the long oaken tables while their masters ate croissants and drank coffee with hot milk and tried to act matter of fact about their dogs and hide the pride in their eyes when they talked about them.

Being at the inn on this special Sunday was suddenly so important to Seppala that he found the courage to approach the widow. "Will you sell the dog?" he asked.

The widow's eyes searched Seppala's face, while she worked gently with the dog. "This is the second time today I have been asked this question. The goat man from Holzheim offered me seventy-five francs."

Seventy-five francs. A fortune!

Seppala was afraid to ask, but he had to. "Did you sell the dog?"

"One does not sell a fine dog so quickly," the widow said. "Well, I cannot stay here all day talking."

Seppala and Claus watched the widow and the dog until they crossed the bridge and were lost behind the church.

"If the goat man offered seventy-five francs, then I must offer her more," Seppala said. "One hundred francs at least."

"How will you get one hundred francs?" Claus asked as they hurried home.

"There must be some way," Seppala said.

11

Dunkel came loping, catching up, begging to play. Seppala threw a stick for him to retrieve. The dog gave chase but his attention was drawn to Frau Snickle's parrot sunning itself in its cage in an open window, and he stopped to yip and bark.

The parrot, quite safe, gave Dunkel a broad piece of its mind.

"What a mongrel Dunkel is," Seppala said, picking up the stick. "He can't concentrate for two seconds."

The boys parted at a beech tree, charred and blackened by lightning, Claus for his home nearby along the stream, and Seppala to his father's wood-carving shop.

Seppala went around to the back garden, slid the bundle of wood from his shoulders and untied the rope. He put the rope into his pocket and stacked the wood on top of a neat pile propped against the house. He noticed that Papa had freshly whitewashed the mirabelle plum tree. Papa, in gardening apron, was turning the plums which were drying on a table in the sun.

"You are late," Papa said, and Seppala followed him onto the porch, where they both washed their hands in a basin.

In the kitchen Mama was ladling soup into blue bowls from a tureen in the center of the table. For once, Annalisa, the baby, was not having her before-dinner cry. No wails came down the stairs from her cradle on the second floor. Papa said grace and they sat down to the meal.

Dunkel came whimpering to the door. Seppala took him

a soupbone. "Why can't you be like the Alsatian?" he asked. "He doesn't tease parrots, or beg for food at mealtime."

Papa broke bread into his soup. "It seems our dinner must be late every day so you can see the widow's dog."

"If I had one hundred francs," Seppala said, "I could buy the Alsatian."

Papa smiled at Mama. "Our son would spend one hundred francs, yet he has not one centime in his pocket."

Mama glanced at Seppala sharply. "If the widow sells her dog, how will she then deliver the casseroles to the weavers?"

"She can get another dog from her brother, the woodsman. He raises and trains them up in the high forest. All I need is one hundred francs."

Papa winked at Mama. "Money, it seems, has a loud voice."

Seppala fished three fat quenelles from his soup and ate them slowly, smacking his lips. "Tomorrow is market day. Surely one of the farmers can use a helper."

Early the next morning Seppala was in the square. Already the farmers had set up their stalls. The dairy farmer had brought cheese from the hills; the vegetable farmers had piled the tables high with carrots, asparagus, potatoes and onions. There were dried apples, rolls of sweet butter, and tubs of Schmierkäse. A live pig squealed in its pen, chickens squawked. There were loaves of black bread and jars of Hagebutten Marmalade to spread on it.

Seppala went first to the Sauerkraut stall. The Kraut farmer's wife had a round red face and a scarf tied under her double chin. "I'm looking for work," Seppala said.

She looked him over. "Turn around," she said. She nodded. "Yah, you are the right size. Now when it comes time to make the Sauerkraut I will put a white suit on you and you can stomp."

"But that won't be until autumn. I need work now."

The Kraut farmer's wife pursed her lips. "Let me think," she said.

Just then Dunkel leapt against Seppala out of nowhere. He licked Seppala's face. Wag . . . wag . . . his tail swept a hill of cabbages piled neatly on the ground. Off rolled the top head. Down tumbled a second. Crash went the hill of cabbages.

"Your dog?" the woman asked tartly.

"No. He follows me around," Seppala said rushing about, picking the cabbages up out of the dust.

They turned back to the stall to discover Dunkel on his hind legs, dirty paws on the scrubbed table, nose sniffing the tub of Sauerkraut.

"Oh Yerra!" the woman cried, banging on the table with a big spoon. "Take him away. Don't come back. Either of you."

Dunkel, ears flattened, tail streaming in the breeze, sailed high over some empty crates and disappeared.

Seppala hurried away.

It took him a few minutes to gather courage to approach Madame LeClerc's flower stand. Madame, a small dark woman, wore a deep shawl and a white cap on her head. She was busy arranging roses in a tub of water. Seppala strode forward briskly so as to make a good impression. But before he could open his mouth, Madame LeClerc's cat arose from its sleep behind a pot of geraniums on the stand, and Seppala heard a growl. He spun around. Dunkel again. The cat arched its back and hissed. Dunkel made a flying leap. The cat took off, the dog after her. Over went the geranium. Seppala picked it up. One of the blooms was broken off.

"Your dog?" Madam LeClerc asked coldly.

"No," Seppala said stoutly. "He follows me."

"You will get a bad reputation, allowing such an untrained animal in your company," Madame said.

Dunkel came bounding back, pleased with himself for having gotten rid of the cat.

Madame grabbed a broom. "Get him out of here," she cried.

Seppala felt ashamed, dragging Dunkel through the marketplace. "Everyone will think you belong to me," he said.

At the edge of the square he let go of the dog. "I can't get a job with you around. Go home, wherever that is," he said, sitting on the curbing.

Dunkel lay down at Seppala's feet, his muzzle on his paws, his eyes closed until Seppala finished his scolding. Then he opened one eye. He looked so funny, Seppala laughed. Dunkel sprang up joyously and licked his face.

Seppala heard Claus' whistle and looked up to see him racing toward them. "I've found a way for you to make one hundred francs," he cried "Follow me!"

He raced ahead to the center of the square. Seppala and Dunkel ran after him. At the bulletin board by the fountain Claus halted and pointed to a notice of the coming Kilbe, the harvest festival. The notice told about the trained seal, the dancing horse . . .

"Here. Here," Claus said, pointing to the bottom of the notice. Seppala read it aloud.

THE ANNUAL SAUSAGE TREE CONTEST WILL
BE HELD AS USUAL. THIS YEAR THE
LORD MAYOR HAS ANNOUNCED AN ADDITIONAL
PRIZE OF 100 FRANCS TO THE PERSON
WHO IS THE FIRST TO REACH THE TIP OF
THE SAUSAGE TREE.

"The Alsatian is practically yours," Claus said. "You are a good tree climber."

"It is just the right amount," Seppala said. "But who has ever been able to reach the top of the sausage tree?"

He remembered the contest from last year and the year before that. The pole, which stood alongside the sidewalk café and was the size of a big tree, was hung with sausages

at various heights. To make the contest more exciting, the pole was greased. No one had ever been known to reach the top.

Seppala knew that the Lord Mayor's one-hundred-franc note was quite safe.

He might as well forget the whole thing.

But he couldn't.

Over the last of his cheese omelette at supper that night he asked Papa about it.

"Climbing the sausage pole is a sport for the older boys and the young men," Papa began.

Seppala held his breath. Papa was going to forbid him to try. Luckily, at that very moment Annalisa began her regular before-feeding crying.

"Seppala, you are finished with supper," Mama said. "Please run upstairs and rock the cradle."

Usually Seppala protested this girls' work, but now he ran to his sister.

Annalisa stopped crying as soon as Seppala began rocking the cradle with his foot. He sat in the window seat looking out into the mirabelle plum tree. Its branches hugged the roof and fingered the window. The tree's newly whitewashed trunk gleamed through the green branches. Just as he heard Claus' whistle below, Seppala thought of something. He leaned out of the window in great excitement and motioned his cousin into their secret meeting place in the crotch of the tree.

Annalisa was cooing contentedly. Quickly, Seppala took a piece of rope from his pocket and tied it to the side of her cradle. He climbed onto the roof, all the while tugging gently at the rope, rocking the cradle. When he reached Claus he blurted: "I've thought of a way to climb the sausage pole."

"How?" Claus asked, breaking a big chunk of Kugelhopf in half and handing Seppala a piece.

Seppala munched the Kuchen and tugged away at the rope. "I'm going to grease the old lightning tree and practice climbing."

Claus let out an appreciative whistle. "I can bring the grease. There's a whole can of it in our stable. When do we start?"

"Tomorrow morning. When I hear the five o'clock bells, I'll climb out my window."

Claus' blue eyes mirrored admiration. "No one will be about then. Even Papa does not bicycle to work until six."

At that moment Annalisa let out an indignant wail.

In his excitement, Seppala had forgotten to tug the rope. He took quick leave, scurried up the tree, up the roof, and through the window in the nick of time, just before Mama opened the door.

The next morning all went well at first. Seppala climbed out the window and down the tree.

There sat Dunkel, eager-eyed and tail-wagging.

"Stay!" Seppala whispered, tiptoeing through the side gate and locking it.

But when he reached the lane where Claus lived, Dunkel came sneaking up behind. So, he had vaulted the gate.

"Don't you understand anything?" Seppala cried.

Dunkel cocked his head to one side and regarded Seppala hopefully.

"All right, as long as you are here, you can come along," Seppala said. "But you are the stupidest dog I ever saw."

Dunkel sprang through the air joyfully. He didn't seem to mind being called stupid if he could just go along.

Claus was waiting at the lightning tree. He began swabbing the trunk with a long-poled greased brush while Seppala put on a pair of discarded trousers he had found in the rag bag.

Now he was ready to begin.

Slip! Slurp! Slide!

He didn't get very far, although he tried over and over.

"You still have plenty of time before the Kilbe," Claus encouraged him.

"I'll practice each morning," Seppala said.

And he did. Each time he tried it, he shinnied himself higher up the slick trunk. The day before the Kilbe he made it to the top. Now he was sure he could climb the sausage pole. He would win the one hundred francs. He would buy the Alsatian. With this handsome dog at his side he would walk into the Tannenbaum Inn on Herren Sonntag. He would be the proudest boy in the valley.

The day of the Kilbe was a holiday for almost everyone. But because Seppala had to rock Annalisa's cradle he was late meeting his Cousin Claus.

"The carpenter's son is home on leave from the Navy," Claus announced when Seppala came out of the house. "On his ship he has learned how to shinny up the mast. Everyone says he will win the one hundred francs."

This was bad news.

The cousins walked glumly down the street, but it was a gay day in the village and soon their high spirits returned. Long tables laden with delicious food lined both sides of the street leading to the square.

There were mounds of marzipan fruits, licorice babies, blocks of dark Schokolade to eat with hunks of crusty white bread.

Seppala and Claus had two coins apiece. There was no hesitation over their first purchase. Each bought a Mannala — a little man made of Lebkuchen. Seppala nibbled on the Mannala's boot, sweet with honey and spiced with ginger. Was there a better taste in all the world? he thought.

It took longer to decide how to spend the second coin. All kinds of booths were set up in the meadow down by the stream. Hawkers shouted their games:

"Hit the running goose and win a life-size doll."

"Throw a ball through the spinning hoop and win a cuckoo clock."

Seppala wanted a cuckoo clock.

But Annalisa did not have a life-size doll.

He picked up a ball and aimed at the goose.

She waddled away at a great pace.

Claus tried it.

He didn't touch a feather.

Now they were penniless.

Overnight a dance floor had been flung over the stream. Already couples were dancing to the music of an accordion.

"There's Dunkel," Claus said, pointing to where the dog was running among the dancing couples who were trying to chase him off the floor.

"Let's run before he sees us," Seppala said.

They sprinted to the sidewalk café where the tables were crowded with villagers gazing up at the sausage tree and making all sorts of predictions as to the day's contest.

Seppala examined the tree from all sides. The easiest sausage to reach was a string of Bratwurst. Farther up hung a Blutwurst. His gaze flickered over the sausages to the broom tied to the top of the pole. To get the one hundred francs he must touch the broom.

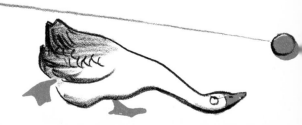

The pole suddenly seemed to stretch to the sky. He wanted to back out. Then he thought of the Alsatian. He would own the dog if he climbed the pole. He knew he must try.

The rumble of a drum announced it was time for the contest.

The villagers crowded around. The people at the sidewalk café stood on chairs. Heads popped out of every window.

The baker's son was the first to try.

He was round and soft as a potato bun. For every inch he gained he slid down two. Finally he landed in a laughing heap on the ground.

The drum rumbled again.

The vintner's son was next. He took a running leap, head down like a billygoat, misjudged the distance, and ran smack into the pole.

"Here is your prize," someone cried, helping him up and presenting him with a dunce cap jingling with bells.

The candlestick maker made it to the Bratwurst. The villagers spurred him on. "Up, Up," they cried. Instead, Bratwurst in hand, he shot downwards. The men slapped their thighs and laughed. The women cried: "Oh Yerra!"

"Make way for the winner," a cocksure voice rang out, and into the circle strode the sailor, light of foot as Madame LeClerc's cat, slim as a willow switch.

He rubbed his hands in the dry dust of the street. He grasped the pole. Up he went — higher and higher —

straight to the Knackwurst, the Mettwurst and the Braunschweiger. He hung the sausages on his arms and around his neck. When he reached the chain of Wienerwurst he threw it grandiosely to a group of children below. They promptly held a tug of war over it.

A ring of Leberwurst was the top sausage. When the sailor reached it he put it on his head. "Hail to the new sausage king," he shouted.

"Hoch!" the villagers cried.

Now the sailor need only to reach up and touch the broom. The contest was almost over.

But the sailor was clowning. Making the most of his newly acquired royalty, he took a kingly bow. Another. He bowed so deeply the sausage crown slid over one eye. He made a grab for it. Whoosh! His feet hit the ground in a cloud of dust.

The men beat each other over the shoulders.

The women held their sides. "Oh Yerra!" they cried.

The Lord Mayor laughed until his stomach shook.

"Well, and who is there left to try for the one hundred francs?" he asked.

Seppala stepped forward.

"A boy!" The Lord Mayor smiled. "But you are too young.

"The rules do not say so," Seppala said.

"Let him try," the villagers cried. "He will not go beyond his own height."

Before they could change their minds, without waiting for the rumble of the drum, Seppala gripped the pole with shins and hands.

Up, up he went. The pole was slick, but not more so than the lightning tree. On and on he went, his eyes steady on the broom.

And then he was at the very top. He touched the broom.

"*Bravo!*" the villagers cried.

He had made it.

He looked down, and when he saw how high up he was he felt dizzy, so he slid down quickly.

Hands reached out to shake his.

The Lord Mayor dug deeply into his pocket. "Here is your prize," he said.

When Seppala felt the one-hundred-franc note in his fist, he thought he must still be at the top of the pole, for his feet surely were not on the ground. He was floating somewhere between earth and sky.

Claus crowded in next to Seppala, and Dunkel leapt up on him. He placed his paws on Seppala's shoulders and licked his face. Seppala rubbed the dog's ear with one hand. With the other he fingered the one-hundred-franc note in his pocket. "Down, Dunkel," he said. "Claus and I have business to attend to."

The two boys, with Dunkel making great leaps between them, ran across the square and along the song-filled streets until they reached the edge of the village and the lane which led to the widow's cottage.

Seppala hammered on the kitchen door. The widow opened the kitchen window and leaned her elbows on the sill.

"I have one hundred francs," Seppala said. "I can pay for the dog."

The widow's answer was drowned in Dunkel's wild barking. He was jumping at the rabbit cages which stood up off the ground. The rabbits cowered in the rear of the cages.

"My Kaninchen," the widow cried. "Oh Yerra!"

Inside the house the Alsatian added his deep bark to the noise and confusion of the yard.

Claus dived for the dog and fell headlong into a bed of bleeding heart.

Seppala grabbed Dunkel and dragged him from the cages.

Still grasping the dog, he stood in front of the widow, ashamed. He saw the coldness in her eyes.

"It takes more than money to buy my dog," she said. "If he is sold it will be to someone responsible. How can I put a trained dog into your care when you allow such a trouble-making nuisance in your company?"

"Dunkel doesn't belong to Seppala." Claus defended his cousin.

"Nevertheless, the dog is constantly with him," the widow said. "So he is his responsibility."

With that she banged down the window and pulled the shade.

The bells in the church tower began the noon Angelus.
The chapel bell from Tannenbaum tinkled softly.
The Klosterglocke in the Hochwald struck the hour.
"Time to go home for dinner," Claus said.
Seppala nodded. They walked without speaking.
Dunkel, tail drooping, kept far, far behind all the way.

Mama and Papa were waiting in the kitchen. They looked stern. So they knew! He might as well tell them the whole story.

Papa's voice when he spoke was more sad than angry. "Perhaps you have learned something this day — that discipline is necessary and good for both man and animal."

"You have a dog who wants to belong to you," Mama said.

"I want a trained dog. Dunkel can't be trained."

Mama started serving the onion pie. "Have you tried?" she asked. "If you truly cared for Dunkel, if you respected him enough to trust him, perhaps he would respond."

No one seemed to understand, Seppala thought. He wanted the beautiful purebred, not the mongrel. How could he take a mongrel into the Tannenbaum Inn? His eyes burned. His throat ached. He couldn't eat.

Upstairs Annalisa sent out a wail.

"I'll rock the cradle," Seppala said, escaping to the stairs.

The next morning when Seppala came outside, Dunkel was, as usual, waiting and jumped on him with dusty paws.

"Down," Seppala said, in no mood to play.

Dunkel just wagged his tail and tried to lick Seppala's face.

"Down," Seppala said again, pushing the dog's shoulders until he lay on the ground.

Dunkel lay quiet but he watched Seppala craftily as he sat on the bottom porch step tying his shoelaces. Then slowly, inch by inch, the dog crept closer until he reached the boy. He sat up, placed a paw on Seppala's knee, cocked his head to one side and looked into the boy's face. This was one of his tricks. It touched Seppala's heart as usual. But this morning he would not let the dog know. "Down," he said, again pushing the dog to the ground.

Dunkel's ears flattened. He put on an injured look. But he made no further move to get up.

Seppala looked at the dog in surprise. Could he be taught? Suddenly, he wanted to find out.

First, Dunkel must have a collar. Papa offered to make one from an old belt. When it was finished, Seppala went out into the yard and fastened it on Dunkel. The dog tried to rid himself of it by rolling in the grass. Finally he gave in and sat quietly.

Seppala took the rope from his pocket and tied it to the collar. Dunkel immediately tried to chew it. He ran about, trying to pull it from Seppala's hands.

"DUNKEL — COME," Seppala said, jerking the rope.

Dunkel stood his ground, defiantly.

"DUNKEL — COME," Seppala commanded, tugging.

Reluctantly, step by step, the dog came until he stood in front of Seppala.

"SIT," Seppala said, leaning forward, pushing the dog into sitting position.

Just then Claus came shouting into the yard. Dunkel broke loose and jumped all over him.

"Don't let him do that," Seppala said. "I'm trying to teach him manners."

But Claus was a softie. He gave Dunkel a cookie and that ended the first lesson.

Later that day, Seppala tried the same command again. The dog was easier to handle. The first time Dunkel came to him willingly without being tugged by the rope, a feeling of triumph shot through Seppala. "Good dog," he said, and Dunkel wagged his tail madly.

Claus tried to help with the training but he wasn't firm enough. He was good at brushing Dunkel and he did it often. "You'll never be as handsome as the Alsatian," he told the dog, "but I'll do the best I can with your plain brown coat."

One day the boys took Dunkel up into the forest. In the clearing by the wayside shrine, Seppala tried to teach him to stay in one place. He ordered Dunkel to lie down.

Dunkel obediently lay at his feet.

"STAY," Seppala commanded.

But Dunkel was distracted by a wood pigeon flying overhead. He jumped up and barked.

Seppala started all over again.

"STAY," he commanded.

A chaffinch sang in a beech tree.

A cowbell tinkled below in the meadow.

Dunkel's tail thumped the ground. He quivered with leashed energy.

Finally he could stand it no longer. He was off, running through the trees.

Claus, dangling from a tree branch, giggled.

Seppala grinned. "Well, Dunkel has learned a few things," he said. Actually, Seppala felt pleased with the dog. For a mongrel, he was learning well. Of course, he couldn't compare in any way with the pure-bred Alsatian.

One chilly, gloomy day, Seppala put Dunkel through his paces again while Claus watched.

Seppala threw a stick to the far end of the yard. Dunkel ran to retrieve it. Seppala held out his hand. "Bring," he said.

Dutifully, Dunkel brought the stick.

"Drop it," Seppala commanded.

Dunkel dropped the stick at Seppala's feet.

"Lie down," Seppala said.

Dunkel obeyed.

"STAY!" Seppala commanded. "STAY!"

He began to walk away from the dog.

Dunkel stayed, but only until Seppala was out of sight behind the woodpile. Then he began inching toward Claus, who sat munching some Kuchen. Claus laughed and Dunkel jumped up and ran to him.

Seppala scolded. "Dunkel, why can't you learn to stay? The Alsatian would stay until he died if necessary."

Dunkel's tail drooped.

Claus shared his Kuchen with the dog.

"The Widow Weiler didn't say Dunkel had to behave like a show dog," Claus said. "All you must do to get her to sell you the Alsatian is to prove you know how to handle a dog so he is not a nuisance."

"You're right," Seppala said. "Let's take Dunkel to the weaving works at noon today to show her what he has learned."

Claus jumped up and ran for the brush. He worked over Dunkel until his coat was glossy.

Seppala hurried into the house and up the stairs to get his one hundred francs.

Back in the yard, he tied the rope to Dunkel's collar. Now they were ready.

The two boys and the dog walked along the cobblestone street. Dunkel almost ignored several cats along the way. He growled only halfheartedly at Frau Snickle's parrot.

The air was cold. Too cold for early autumn. "It looks like rain," Claus said.

Seppala knew it was high time he talked business with the Widow Weiler if he was to walk into the Tannenbaum Inn on Men's Sunday with the Alsatian. The big day was almost here. Soon the snows would close the paths to the Inn. Even now the biting wind had the feel of winter.

Dunkel walked close to Seppala, brushing against his leg. All at once Seppala felt sad, without reason. He stopped to pet the dog before going on.

As they crossed the stream the bittersweet notes of a yellowhammer came to them from a willow tree. "The last bird to sing before a storm," Claus said and both boys looked up at the darkening sky.

Now they could see the widow in front of the weaving works. The Alsatian was unharnessed and the widow was holding him by the collar, while she spoke to a stranger.

"It's the goat man," Claus said. "The one who wants to buy the Alsatian."

"Maybe we're too late," Seppala said, beginning to walk faster.

But Dunkel held back.

Seppala pulled on the rope. "What's the matter with you?" he asked.

The bells in the Storkheim church tower began to ring

the Angelus and the weavers streamed out of the factory.

The goat man turned and saw Dunkel.

Dunkel began growling, deep-throated, ominous.

"Where did you get him?" the goat man shouted in an ugly voice, pointing to Dunkel.

"He came into the village," Seppala said.

"You stole him. He's my property. I would know that dark coat anyplace."

Dunkel's ears flattened, his hackles raised. He strained to get away.

The goat man came closer and he made a grab for the dog's collar.

Dunkel bared his teeth. It took all of Seppala's strength to hold him.

The goat man looked frightened. He began to back away.

Dunkel, wild now, pulled himself free from Seppala. The dog stood facing the goat man, who kept backing toward the factory door. "Keep him. He's a savage wolf," he shouted.

Dunkel leapt high over the widow's cart. The rope dangling from his collar caught on a wheel of the cart, tipping it over. Casseroles flew in all directions. Coffee spilled over the cobblestones. Wine bottles broke.

"Oh Yerra!" the widow cried, holding fast to the Alsatian.

"Oh Yerra!" the workers cried.

The goat man disappeared into the factory just an instant before Dunkel hurled himself against the closed door.

"Dunkel! Dunkel!" Seppala shouted, running to him.

But Dunkel, rope streaming behind him, took off like a cannonball up toward the forest.

Seppala ran after him.

"Wait for me," Claus cried, racing after Seppala. The dog was already out of sight.

"What made him do it?" Claus gasped, catching up.

Seppala shook his head. He put his hands in his pockets. His fingers touched the one-hundred-franc note. Would it pay for the damage?

Strange, but he felt no anger toward the dog. "He must have had a good reason for going after the goat man," he said.

"I'll bet the goat man did own Dunkel," Claus said. "Remember, when we first saw the dog he had been hurt. He cowered. I'll bet the goat man beat him."

"You're right," Seppala said. "That's why Dunkel ran away from him, and that's why Dunkel went after him today."

Seppala walked faster. He must find the dog. "Dunkel!" he shouted. "Dunkel!"

Claus whistled.

There was no answering bark.

It was getting colder. The boys buttoned their jackets and climbed higher into the forest. When they reached the clearing by the mountain shrine, a few snowflakes drifted down.

Claus was excited about the first snow. He ran around in circles. He held back his head and tried to catch some snowflakes in his mouth.

Seppala cupped his hands around his lips. "Dunkel! Dunkel!" he shouted.

The snow was falling more thickly now.

Claus walked backwards in it, making patterns with his feet.

And then, all of a sudden, close by the shrine, they saw Dunkel. Motionless. Head held proudly. Waiting.

Seppala knelt and held out his hand.

The dog leapt into his arms.

Claus whooped for joy. He made a running leap at a low-hanging branch of a fir tree and swung from it.

"We'd better start down, Claus," Seppala said, rubbing Dunkel's ears, hugging the dog, letting him lick his face.

There was the sharp retort of a branch snapping. Something falling.

Dunkel stiffened.

"Claus, let's go," Seppala cried.

There was no answer.

The clearing was hushed, white, empty.

Dunkel raced to its edge. His bark was one of warning and Seppala hurried after him.

Some ten feet below the edge of the cliff, on a ledge
which hung in space over a gorge, lay Claus, motionless.

Seppala picked his way down to his cousin. As he knelt beside him, Claus opened his eyes and tried to sit up. "My leg — there's something wrong."

The leg was bent grotesquely. Seppala knew it was important that Claus lie still. "I'll get help," he said.

Claus turned his head and looked far below into the whitened trees. "I can crawl back up the cliff . . ."

"No, no," Seppala said. "Lie still. You might hurt yourself more. I'll run fast."

Claus didn't answer. Seppala knew his cousin was afraid here, and he thought of all the things that might happen if Claus moved.

Dunkel brushed up against Seppala's leg. The dog had followed. He stood over Claus now, whimpering.

Dunkel!

Dunkel could stay with Claus. His cousin would not be alone then.

Seppala knew he must trust the dog. He grasped him by the collar and maneuvered him close to the edge of the ledge.

"DUNKEL — LIE DOWN," Seppala said.

The dog did as he was told.

Now if Claus raised his head he would see the dog, not the deep gorge. He wouldn't be afraid to wait for help to come. He wouldn't be alone.

Seppala took off his coat and spread it over his cousin. "Dunkel will stay with you," he said.

"No he won't," Claus said. "He never does what I tell him. He'll follow you."

"He will stay," Seppala said.

He put his hand on Dunkel's head. "Stay close to Claus. Keep him warm. STAY! STAY!"

Seppala scrambled up the cliff and looked down. Through the snowflakes Dunkel stared up at him. "STAY!" he commanded. "STAY! STAY!"

Seppala began to run.

He did not look back to see if Dunkel was following. Dunkel *had* to stay.

By the time Seppala came out of the forest, the sudden storm had halted.

He took the shortcut to the village.

He ran home and told Papa and Mama.

Mama hurried to Tante.

Papa ran to get Herr Doktor.

Soon everyone was ready.

Seppala led the way up the mountain path.

Papa was right behind him, carrying blankets.

Herr Doktor had his bag of medicines.

Tante carried a hot toddy.

Someone brought a stretcher.

Seppala's heart pounded as he ran. Had Dunkel really stayed? Had he protected Claus?

When Seppala reached the shrine, he was afraid to look over the side of the cliff.

When he did his heart leapt.

Dunkel had stayed! He was down there beside Claus, muzzle on Claus' shoulder.

The others caught up. It seemed no time at all until the nightmare was over. Claus was carried up the cliff and down into the village. The Herr Doktor put Claus' leg in a large white plaster cast. Claus was proud of it.

Of course everyone in Storkheim heard about the accident, and about Dunkel.

The Kraut farmer's wife came to Seppala's home with a crock of Sauerkraut.

The baker brought a basket of croissants.

The Widow Weiler came. She brought the Alsatian. "You may buy him," she said to Seppala. "You proved you know how to bring out the best in a dog."

Seppala looked at the handsome Alsatian. The purebred. He was being offered everything he had thought he wanted.

But he already had what he wanted.

"Thank you," he said. "I have a dog."

The widow smiled. "I thought as much," she said. "I have brought you a harness for Dunkel."

The harness had two bells on the front. Seppala had never seen one as handsome. He was speechless.

Papa grinned. "It seems I will have to build a cart."

"And paint it blue," Mama said.

The Lord Mayor was the next to call.

"Seppala, will you and your dog be my guests at the Tannenbaum Inn next Sunday?" he asked.

"Shall we go?" Seppala asked Dunkel, who was sitting at his feet.

Dunkel wagged his tail so hard he rocked Annalisa's cradle.

"We accept," Seppala said.

Breakfast at the Tannenbaum Inn on Herren Sonntag was all Seppala had dreamed it would be. Men and boys from Storkheim and Oberheim and St. Philippe came walking along mountain paths to the inn.

Seppala did not have to tie his dog outside with the nuisances. He took Dunkel right into the inn and the dog lay under the table dignified and proud, even when the four cuckoo clocks chattered at once.

The Lord Mayor smiled all around, pleased to be seen in the company of a boy with such a famous dog.

Seppala ate his croissants and drank the hot milk, coffee-flavored. He looked out the windows to all the Vogesens, the layered green mountains that stretched as far as the eye could see. He pretended to be absorbed in the beautiful scene when, in fact, he was bursting with pride of Dunkel.

But of course he must not show it.

A true master of his dog never did.

FOREIGN WORDS

(P) Patois — Alsatian   (G) German   (F) French

Storkheim	(G)	Storkhome
Schneeglöckchen	(G)	snowdrops
Primel	(G)	primroses
Tannenbaum	(G)	fir tree
Klosterglocke	(G)	convent bell
Hochwald		High Forest
Herren Sonntag	(G)	Gentlemen's Sunday
Dunkel	(G)	Dark
Uf de Berge isch gut wohne	(P)	Up the mountains is good living (literal translation)
Holzheim	(G)	Woodhome
franc	(F)	French coin
Frau Snickle	(G)	Married Woman (Mrs. Snickle)
centime	(F)	French coin
quenelles	(F)	dumplings
Schmierkäse	(G)	soft cheese, as cottage cheese
Hagebutten	(G)	butter made from rose hips, the brightly colored fruit of the hedge rose
Yah!	(G)	yes
Oh Yerra!	(P)	Alsation expression denoting joy, surprise or calamnity, depending on inflection used.
Madame LeClerc	(F)	Married Woman (Mrs. LeClerc)
Kilbe	(P)	Festival held at harvest time
Kugelhopf	(P)	Alsatian yeast cake
Kuchen	(G)	cake
Schokolade	(G)	chocolate
Mannala	(P)	cookie in shape of man (gingerbread boy)
Lebkuchen	(G)	cookie made with ginger and other spices
vintner	(F)	winemaker
Bratwurst	(G)	small German sausage
Blutwurst	(G)	hog's pudding sausage
Knackwurst	(G)	highly seasoned dried sausage
Leberwurst	(G)	liver sausage
Mettwurst	(G)	bologna
Braunschweiger	(G)	smoked liver sausage
Wienerwurst	(G)	small Vienna sausages — wieners
Hoch!	(G)	high (a salute or a cheer)
Kaninchen	(G)	rabbits
chaffinch		small European chaff-eating songbird
yellowhammer		small European finch with yellow head, neck and breast
Tante	(F & G)	aunt
Herr Doktor	(G)	Mr. Doctor
croissants	(F)	crescent-shaped butter rolls